MW00949089

My Way
A mi manera

A Margaret and Margarita Story

Un cuento de Margarita y Margaret

LYNN REISER

Greenwillow Books, *An Imprint of* HarperCollins*Publishers*

I am almost ready.

Ya casi estoy lista.

This is me, Margaret.
I like to do things
my way.

Ésta soy yo, Margarita.
Me gusta hacer las cosas
a mi manera.

This is how I fix my hair.
I like to fix it my way.

Así es como me gusta peinarme.
Me gusta peinarme a mi manera.

This is what I like to wear.
I like to wear it my way.

Así es como me gusta vestirme.
Me gusta vestirme a mi manera.

This is how I greet my friends.

Así es como saludo a mis amigos.

This is how I make my art.

Así es como hago mi arte.

This is what I eat for lunch.

Esto es lo que almuerzo.

And this is how I take my nap.
I like to do things my way.

Y así es como duermo mi siesta.
Me gusta hacer las cosas a mi manera.

But sometimes . . .

Pero a veces . . .

I like to
fix my hair
and wear my clothes
and greet my friends
and make my art
and eat my lunch
and take my nap
your way.

Me gusta
peinarme
y vestirme
y saludar a mis amigos
y hacer mi arte
y comer mi almuerzo
y dormir mi siesta
a tu manera.

And sometimes . . .

Y a veces . . .

I like to
fix my hair,
wear my clothes,
greet my friends,
make my art,
eat my lunch,
and take my nap
both ways.

me gusta
peinarme,
vestirme,
saludar a mis amigos,
hacer mi arte,
comer mi almuerzo
y dormir mi siesta
de ambas maneras.

Sometimes
I like to do things
my way.
Sometimes
I like to do things
your way.
Sometimes
I like
to do things
both ways . . .

A veces
me gusta hacer las cosas
a mi manera.
A veces
me gusta hacer las cosas
a tu manera.
A veces
me gusta
hacer las cosas
de ambas maneras . . .

But I
ALWAYS
like to do them
with you!

Pero
SIEMPRE
me gusta hacer las cosas
contigo!

Thank you!
¡Gracias!
Good-bye!
Adiós, Margarita
y mama de Margarita.

¡Gracias!
Thank you!
¡Adiós!
Good-bye, Margaret
and Margaret's mama.

¡Hasta mañana!

See you tomorrow!

To Susan R., with love

Thanks to Barbara Mergen Alvarado, Jesús Alvarado, Clara Giraudo, Nancy Moscoso-Guzmán, Graziella Patrucco de Solodow, Joseph B. Solodow, and Raul Verduzco for their thoughtful and meticulous attention to finding exactly the right Spanish words.

 www.harpercollinschildrens.com
Rayo is an imprint of HarperCollins Publishers, Inc. Watercolor and black ink were used to prepare the full-color art. The text type is Polymer Book Roman.

Library of Congress Cataloging-in-Publication Data Reiser, Lynn. My way = A mi manera/ by Lynn Reiser. p. cm.
"Greenwillow Books." Summary: Parallel text in Spanish and English portrays Margaret and Margarita, who mirror one another as they fix their hair, greet their friends, and engage in other routine activities, each in her own special way. ISBN-10: 0-06-084101-X (trade bdg.) ISBN-13: 978-0-06-084101-0 (trade bdg.) [1. Individuality—Fiction. 2. Spanish language materials—Bilingual.] I. Title: A mi manera. II. Title. PZ73.R414 2006 [E]—dc22 2005035646 First Edition 10 9 8 7 6 5 4 3 2 1

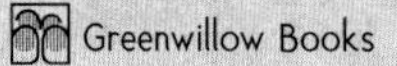